Follies & Foibles: A Sweet "Pride & Prejudice" Variation

Abbey North

Published by Abbey North JAFF Books, 2022.

This is a work of fiction. Similarities to real people, places, or events are entirely coincidental.

FOLLIES & FOIBLES: A SWEET "PRIDE & PREJUDICE" VARIATION

First edition. July 28, 2022.

Copyright © 2022 Abbey North.

ISBN: 979-8215555651

Written by Abbey North.

Blurb

While in Kent, Fitzwilliam finds the object of his affection in attendance at Hunsford. Interaction deepens his interest, and he's prepared to throw aside caution and common sense to claim Elizabeth Bennet as his bride. On the cusp of proposing, they end up arguing instead when she learns about his meddling to keep Bingley safe from Jane. While fleeing him, Lizzy is injured, and he carries her to Rosings Park. It is the beginning of a new understanding between them.

It's also the beginning of a friendship between Lizzy and Anne, and Fitzwilliam finds himself drawn into Lizzy's madcap scheme to ensure his cousin's happiness. An unintended engagement requires maneuvers and machinations, but it might provide Fitzwilliam the perfect opportunity to enact his own agenda—one that leads to a life of happiness with one stubborn Miss Bennet.

Chapter One

Fitzwilliam knew it was madness, but he could no longer deny how he felt about Miss Elizabeth Bennet. His feelings had been building for months, ever since that disaster of a meeting at the Assembly ball. He recalled the time she'd spent confined at Netherfield while waiting for Miss Jane's illness to pass, and where he had once cringed at their interactions, now he smiled fondly.

It was there he had first gotten to see the real Miss Bennet, and he marveled now that he had been blind to her for any length of time. Of course, her atrocious family was still a consideration, and it had allowed him to continue to fight his feelings for longer. He had fled Netherfield with every intention of never seeing her again, but when she'd arrived at Hunsford a few weeks ago, having already been in attendance when he and his cousin Richard came to visit Lady Catherine, it had seemed like fate.

Fitzwilliam was many things, but he wasn't one who could defy fate. He could see now that he was destined to be with Miss Bennet, and he only hoped he could convince her of the truth of that. Surely, she could not remain unmoved in his presence? He had seen glances she directed his way when she thought he wasn't looking, and he certainly hadn't imagined the becoming flush and coy smile on her face yesterday evening when he sat across from her in the dining room at Rosings Park when their gazes had locked. There had been such an air of softness about her for a moment, and it had fueled his resolve that he simply must confess his feelings and plead for her hand.

He was certain his aunt would be dismayed, and the Matlocks would probably find her equally unsuitable, but none of that swayed Fitzwilliam any longer. He was prepared to accept her and overlook the unsuitability of her family, and surely, she would be nothing but grateful for his willingness to lower himself.

He stopped by the rectory, impatient to meet with her though visiting hours hadn't yet begun. Mrs. Collins seemed surprised to see him, but she directed him to the grounds, along with an airy, "Eliza does like to walk every morning, whether she is at home or here." There was a gleam of interest in Mrs. Collins' eyes, but he didn't indulged her curiosity. Instead, he rushed from the rectory and set out to find Miss Bennet.

Finally, he saw her figure ahead of him, and he increased his pace, stumbling for a moment as he realized she was walking with his cousin. Miss Bennet had her arm through Richard's, and she appeared to be engrossed in whatever his cousin was saying. A sharp sting of jealousy twinged through him, and he gritted his teeth as he hurried forward.

Miss Bennet's dowery would never be sufficient for his cousin, and he refused to allow the man to toy with her affections. Those affections belonged solely to Fitzwilliam, and he had no doubt Miss Bennet would acknowledge that fact as soon as he proposed.

As he drew closer, Richard was the first to notice him. He stopped walking and lifted his hand in greeting, but he appeared awkward. "Fitzwilliam, I did not expect to see you out and about so early."

He frowned at his cousin. "I am often up with the dawn."

"Er, right." Richard scratched at his neck in an uneasy fashion, and he appeared discomforted. "Still, you are not one for long walks in the mornings. I would be much less surprised to see you on Goliath."

Normally, he would've claimed the horse for a morning ride, but recalling Miss Bennet had a fear of them, he had eschewed his usual mode of transport. He just shrugged his shoulders without bothering to reply. He turned to Miss Bennet then. "I was hoping we might walk together for a time, Miss Bennet. There is something I wish to discuss with you."

"Oh, how fortuitous. There is something I wish to discuss with you too." Despite her eager words, her tone sounded off to him.

As he looked closer, he realized she was almost trembling, and she seemed angry. He glared at his cousin, wondering what Richard had done to leave the lady in such a state. He would never expect Richard to do something dishonorable, but he couldn't deny ugly thoughts came to him. In a stiff tone, he said, "You will excuse us then, Richard." He made it a statement of fact rather than a question.

The colonel hesitated for a moment, looking like he wanted to say something. He slanted a glance to Lizzy, clearly finding her resolved, and then he sighed heavily. "Yes, of course, Fitzwilliam." There was an air of inevitability about him as he dropped Miss Bennet's arm and stepped away.

Fitzwilliam watched him go, unsurprised when his cousin paused and looked back once before continuing onward as Fitzwilliam offered his arm to Miss Bennet. To his surprise, she shunned it. After an awkward second, he returned it to his side and cleared his throat. "What I wish to discuss with you..." He trailed off, finding it unexpectedly more difficult to begin now that they were alone. "Let us walk."

She nodded stiffly and fell into step beside him, but she still didn't lift her arm to take his, though he made a pointed effort to offer it. Finally, he let it drop to his side again. "I hope Richard did not upset you."

She looked up, eyes wide. "Why would you assume that?"

"The situation seemed tense between you, and he clearly left you in that state. I hope you did not have your hopes pinned on him offering for you, Miss Bennet." He couldn't help a sharp note of censure bleeding through, feeling betrayed by the idea of Miss Bennet pinning her cap for his cousin. "He is the second son of an Earl, so he must have an heiress to maintain his current lifestyle should he ever wish to retire from the militia."

She frowned at him, looking perplexed. "I am aware. I have no designs on your cousin, I assure you, Mr. Darcy." She scowled, looking angry.

He put up a hand, realizing he might have sounded accusatory. "I was not saying you did. I was merely explaining the situation. I hope you would have no reason to look at Richard in such a way."

Lizzy shrugged her shoulders. "He is a fine young man, and he will make an excellent husband for a lucky heiress, but I understand the reality of the situation."

He disliked hearing her speak so flatteringly of his cousin, though Fitzwilliam knew the colonel was a fine man indeed. He wasn't so far gone as to not realize jealousy was prompting his negative reaction to her faint praise.

He cleared his throat, determined to set aside that topic of conversation and focus on what he had come to discuss. "We have known each other for a few months now, Miss Bennet." He hesitated, waiting until she had nodded before he continued. "I must admit, we did not get off to a good start."

She let out a decidedly unladylike snort. "No, we did not. Your way of insulting every woman in Meryton ensured that." She grimaced lightly. "Except Jane."

"Y-yes I... I do owe you an apology for that." Why would she bring that up once more? He was content to let it never be mentioned between them again. "As we have spent much time together—"

"Not overly much, yet it has an uncanny ability to feel like forever." Her tone was difficult to read.

He frowned, feeling a dart of apprehension. "Yes, I suppose that is true. Conceivably that is why I feel so confident in discussing this with you. Though we have not spent perhaps as much time as other couples, I feel like we have a good basis. I recognize your flaws, and I understand and accept the burden of your family. I know this is typically not done, but I have decided to be happy and not worry so much about what is acceptable or not."

She seemed mystified. "How very wonderful for you. While you have decided to be happy, I must ask, why have you gone out of your way to ensure others remain unhappy?"

Her tone was entirely too sweet, and it caused him to stumble over his words and his feet. He drew to a stop as he looked at her. "Pardon me, but I do not understand the question, Miss Bennet."

She had stopped as well, and now she turned to fully face him, hands on her hips. "Have you been trying to prevent Mr. Bingley from courting my dear sister, Jane?"

Fitzwilliam gulped. "How did you hear about that?"

"Your cousin was most enlightening, though I suspect he did not realize he was being so at first. He simply mentioned how you had to save your friend from a grasping social climber. When I ventured to guess it might be Mr. Charles Bingley, he confirmed it, and he seemed to realize I was upset by the news, though perhaps not why. No doubt, he is not yet aware Jane is the target of your villainy."

He drew himself up, anger filling him. "It is not villainous to wish to protect a friend. Your sister is all the things you said and more. I overheard her conversation with your mother."

She frowned. "I do not need to know which one, for any would be damning, but I implore you to consider whether you heard Jane or my mother advocating for the mercenary position of marrying Mr. Bingley solely for his four thousand per year?"

Fitzwilliam frowned and then shrugged. "It does not matter. It is obvious Miss Jane does not have the full regard she should for Bingley. He deserves a love match, not a woman in love with his fortune and station in life. I have been nothing but protective of him."

"In the process, you have broken my sister's heart by providing unneeded protection. She loves Bingley, you cad."

His shoulders reared back, and his anger reached new heights. "She does not. It is obvious to—"

"What is obvious is you are a man who likes the sound of his own voice and would never reconsider his opinion. I assume that once someone has lost your good opinion, it is lost forever?"

He nodded stiffly. "That is a fair assessment."

"I assure you, you are not the only one to hold that position, Mr. Darcy. I do not believe I could find a lower opinion of you if I tried. I cannot believe you would willingly consign my sister to a broken heart because she is shy and not as expressive with her emotions as you would have her be. Have you even discussed it with Mr. Bingley? Do you know if she shows a different side to him?"

He scowled. "I do not have to know these things. It is evident from observation that she does not love him. I will not allow Bingley to waste his heart and fortune on a woman such as she. Your family alone would preclude her from being a suitable match for Bingley, and he is but one generation removed from trade."

As he spoke, Fitzwilliam was forced to acknowledge the truth of that. If the Bennets were too low for his friend Bingley to consider a match, Fitzwilliam must remember the same for himself. He suddenly realized the folly of what he had come to do, and it was like a dash of cold water in his face, bringing clarity and comprehension once more. He absolutely could not be in love with Miss Bennet, but if he were silly enough to indulge in that folly, he could allow it to go no farther than a private indulgence. He simply must not ask for her hand.

That didn't seem to be a concern anyway, for she was clearly enraged. She glared at him and turned to storm away.

"The discussion is not over," he called after her.

She turned to look at him, glaring with unfettered heat. "I cannot stand to look at you for one more moment, let alone hear another word escape your mouth, Mr. Darcy." With a nod for emphasis, she turned around and kept striding away.

He had to admit it would've been a grand exit, save for the fact that in her anger and haste, Miss Bennet grew clumsy. With a sharp cry, she pitched forward, hitting the ground with a thud he could hear even from there before she started to roll down the hill.

In alarm, he rushed after her. Though they had been exchanging angry words, he felt nothing but concern as he caught up with Miss Bennet, who laid at the bottom of the hill in a crumpled heap.

Chapter Two

Lizzy was aware of Mr. Darcy bending down beside her, but she was still too stunned to speak or respond to his attempts to get her attention. Her head was throbbing where she had banged it against the ground, and it matched an echoing pain in her ankle. As he offered a hand, awareness started to return. When he put his hands on her arms, she jerked away. "Do not touch me."

His lips compressed, but he seemed determined to ignore her outburst. "I am only going to assist you, Miss Bennet."

With a grudging nod, mainly because she wasn't certain she could fully gain her feet on her own with her head still spinning and pounding, Lizzy groaned, because the motion made the world spin around her. She made a mental note not to do that again as he carefully lifted her to her feet. This close to him, for a moment she could allow herself to enjoy his proximity, finding it easier to contemplate with her head aching and making it impossible to focus on all the reasons she disliked Mr. Darcy.

When she felt steady enough, she started to jerk away from him. His hands had barely moved when her ankle collapsed, and she would've fallen again if not for his quick thinking. He embraced her, keeping her standing before lifting her into his arms.

Lizzy let out a squeal of outrage. "Put me down at once, Mr. Darcy."

"Be still, Miss Bennet. You clearly cannot walk on your own." He sounded stiff and strained, and he glared down at her in a way meant to silence her.

Lizzy decided to ignore that, continuing to protest as he carried her, but she couldn't put up much of a physical fight. Her head was still hurting too much, and from just the brief moment when she'd tried to stand on her own, she knew her ankle wouldn't allow her to walk all the way back to Hunsford. As much as she bitterly resented having to take his help, Lizzy knew she must.

Still, she did enjoy making him slightly miserable in the process as she continued to drone on about how she could handle it on her own and insist he put her down. Of course, being the obstinate man he was, Darcy made no attempt to do so. He continued to carry her, and Lizzy burned with embarrassment as they approached Rosings Park.

Anyone might see this spectacle. It was not enough to force them to become engaged, but it would still set tongues wagging. She would much prefer people discuss how much of a klutz she was over speculating there was some great romance between her and Mr. Darcy. The idea was laughable, though she found no humor in it. Instead, it caused a vague, melancholic ache in her chest that she had difficulty understanding or explaining.

"We will send for the apothecary to examine you," said Mr. Darcy in a firm tone.

Lizzy frowned at the thought, wanting to protest, though recognizing perhaps she shouldn't. She decided her head was aching enough that she could fall silent. As fun as it was to continue to castigate Mr. Darcy for his interference, it was making her head hurt worse. Regretfully, she decided to abandon her mission.

Instead, Lizzy allowed herself a moment to indulge in the experience of being carried by someone. She hadn't experienced such a thing since she was a little girl, and having Mr. Darcy hold her like this certainly didn't make her feel childlike in any fashion. It caused a strange tingling in her body and a sharp awareness of just how close he was.

She inhaled without thought, enjoying his brisk male scent that was uniquely him, underscored with peppermint and perhaps pine. Something fresh and outdoorsy.

With her eyes closed, Lizzy wasn't paying much attention, but they snapped open abruptly when she heard his feet clicking on marble. She gasped when she realized he'd brought her into Rosings Park instead of taking her the rest of the distance to Hunsford. "What are you doing?"

"I am ensuring you are settled before sending for the apothecary, madam." He spoke as though she were a simple child.

She rolled her eyes. "We have already established that plan, but why am I in Rosings Park?"

"It is considerably closer than Hunsford, and you should be settled quickly."

She shook her head and then winced as she did so. It caused a sloshy feeling and an accompanying twist of nausea in her stomach. "I insist you take me to Hunsford at once, Mr. Darcy."

"I insist you must remain here, for that is an extra distance to carry you that is unrequired."

Her mouth snapped shut, and she wasn't certain if she should be insulted by the implication that she was too heavy to carry, or if she should immediately assume he had intended to insult her. Perhaps he was only thinking of her, but she quickly discarded the idea. Mr. Darcy appeared to be a man who only thought of himself and those important to him, and Lizzy certainly wasn't in that category.

She could have continued to protest, but her stomach and head were working in conjunction, trying to undo her, and she realized the unpleasant sloshy feeling was worse each time Mr. Darcy took a step. It would be a relief not to have to be carried any farther, and she could always move to Hunsford as soon as the apothecary had seen her. Mr. Collins could send his wagon, or Mr. Darcy surely had a coach if Lady Catherine refused the use of hers.

Lizzy doubted the older woman would do such a thing, for she wished to appear a gracious hostess—as long as one fell in line as a guest and agreed with everything she said. Recalling that she had dared contradict Lady Catherine's opinions on a few occasions, she had cause to wonder if perhaps Darcy's aunt might withhold the carriage after all. That was a problem to worry about after she'd seen the apothecary.

As Mr. Darcy settled her into a guestroom upstairs, Lizzy heard a gasp from the doorway. She turned her head and saw Miss Anne standing there, looking perplexed and a little scandalized. "It is not what you think," she said quickly.

After a moment, Miss Anne entered the room, ignoring Lizzy's comment as she looked at her cousin. "Whatever is happening, Fitzwilliam?"

"Miss Bennet tripped and injured herself. We were closer to Rosings Park than Hunsford, and I am about to send for the apothecary. Will you wait with her?"

Miss Anne immediately nodded, taking a seat beside the bed as Fitzwilliam stood up. He left the room without a word, and Lizzy did her best to rearrange herself so that she was somewhat comfortable. She was surprised when Miss Anne stood up and lifted pillows off the nearby divan, using them to raise her ankle.

Anne smiled at her in the process. "I once sprained my ankle, and Mama's physician told me to keep my foot above the level of my heart to reduce swelling."

"Thank you. It is not something of which I was aware." She cleared her throat. "How did you sprain your ankle?"

"It was one of the few times when I managed to escape my governess and play outdoors. Unfortunately, I injured myself in the process, which required a search of the grounds to find me. I was unable to bring myself back, you see? It cemented my mother's determination that I must remain indoors to protect my health." She sighed heavily. "Tell me, how did you find yourself in such a predicament, Miss Bennet?"

"I tripped and fell down a hill." Lizzy omitted the rest of the story.

"How did Fitzwilliam come to find you?" There was a hint of speculation in her gaze.

Lizzy recalled then that Lady Catherine wanted her daughter and nephew to marry. Was Miss Anne agreeable to the idea as well? It seemed unlikely that she wouldn't be, so Lizzy wondered if she was jealous. She hastened to assure her there was no reason to be. "He happened to come across me and offered his assistance. It was dreadfully embarrassing for both of us."

Anne surprised her by smiling then. "I seriously doubt that, for Fitzwilliam seemed quite happy to have you in his arms even under the circumstances."

Lizzy frowned, uncertain about the other woman's meaning. "I do not understand."

Anne didn't reply, but she had a knowing expression, and her lips remained curved into a slight smile that didn't flee until the imperious voice of Lady Catherine broke the quiet.

Lizzy tensed, noticing Anne had done the same, as Lady Catherine entered the room. She stared at Lizzy aghast for a moment. "Whatever is going on here, Miss Bennet?"

"Miss Bennet has been injured," said Anne quickly. "Fitzwilliam brought her here after finding her, since it was closer than Hunsford. He has gone for the apothecary."

Lady Catherine scowled. "You were alone with my nephew?"

Lizzy hastily lifted a hand. "He came to my assistance and nothing more, Lady Catherine. He was quite gallant." She practically had to choke out the word, recalling the argument that had prompted her injury to start with.

How she burned at having to take the blame for the accident without being able to implicate Mr. Darcy's role in it. Yet, that was a better alternative than having anyone know they had been alone together and arguing before she so foolhardily rushed away from him.

After a moment, Lady Catherine's ire seemed to flee, and her expression became more gracious—at least as gracious as it ever could,

Lizzy imagined. "Yes, you must stay until the apothecary has ruled you fit to leave. It is our Christian duty, is it not?"

Lizzy had to suppress the urge to roll her eyes at the condescension. She managed what she hoped was a semi-convincing smile and polite tone when she said, "My gratitude knows no bounds."

As she glanced over at Anne, Lizzy didn't miss the way the woman's lips twitched, and she clearly caught Lizzy's hint of sarcasm.

Fortunately, Lady Catherine appeared inured against it, for she simply nodded and held herself with the bearing of a queen. "We embrace our duties and burdens in this household. I shall leave you to it, but I will send up a maid, so my daughter is not having to play nursemaid."

"I do not mind, Mama," said Anne softly.

Lady Catherine scowled. "It is beneath you, child, and it is time for your afternoon nap." She spoke with a note of authority that dared Anne to defy it.

With a small sigh, Anne got to her feet. She looked at Lizzy, patting her hand for a moment. "I have no doubt the apothecary will be here shortly, and you shall be fine, Miss Bennet."

"No doubt. Thank you for your kindness, Miss Anne, and you as well, Lady Catherine." She sounded slightly less sincere when she tacked on the last part of the statement and looked at Lady Catherine, who was paying her no mind anyway. She could have saved the courtesies, though good manners were ingrained in her.

Once they had left, Lizzy allowed her eyes to close. The room was still spinning around her, and her head ached dreadfully yet. She vaguely heard someone take a seat nearby, and she peeled open one eyelid to identify a maid who had taken up her post. Lizzy closed her eyes again, wanting to be left alone rather than have the maid fuss over her. The girl seemed content with her embroidery anyway.

Lizzy must have dozed off, because she woke with a start sometime later, feeling a cool hand against her forehead. She opened her eyes to find a kindly visage above her belonging to an older man. He had an impressive white mustache that could have been alive all on its own.

"Good afternoon, Miss Bennet. It is a pleasure to meet you."

His kindly face and the genuine warmth in his voice made it impossible not to smile despite how wretched she felt. "It is lovely to meet you as well, though I do not know your name, sir."

Mr. Darcy cleared his throat then, making Lizzy aware he was still in the room. "Allow me to present Miss Elizabeth Bennet, Mr. Dennison. Miss Bennet, this is Mr. Dennison, the local apothecary."

"Mr. Darcy has been quite concerned about you," said Mr. Dennison. He frowned slightly as he looked into her eyes, peeling them up in an uncomfortable way. "Do follow the track of my finger, Miss Bennet." As he spoke, he lifted his index finger on his left hand and started moving it back and forth and up and down. Lizzy did her best to follow it, though it made her head hurt worse and increased her nausea. With a groan, she closed her eyes when he dropped his hand.

"Yes, you do have a concussion. You also sprained your ankle. Whomever propped up your foot has undoubtedly assisted with the healing."

Lizzy managed to open her eyes again. "How long until I feel better, Mr. Dennison?"

"I imagine the head will improve within three to four days, and likely your ankle will be better around the same time. After that, once you feel confident putting weight upon it, and your headache has faded to a tolerable level, you can get out of bed."

Lizzy scowled. "I am afraid I cannot remain in bed. For one thing, I do not live at Rosings Park. I am visiting Hunsford."

The apothecary nodded. "Yes, I have heard Mr. Collins discuss his wife's visitor. I inferred you must be her."

"So you can see why I must return to the rectory."

The older man frowned. "It would be ill advised to move just yet. You are much better off where you are, Miss Bennet."

"We shall ensure she stays there and has good care," said Mr. Darcy firmly

Lizzy huffed a sigh of impatience. "Would you please send for Charlotte, Mr. Darcy?"

"I shall." He turned and left the room, allowing Mr. Dennison to finish with her. The apothecary gave her a few vials of medication to control her nausea and help with the pain, and then he departed.

Lizzy had barely been alone for a few minutes when Charlotte appeared, looking frantic with worry. Her friend rushed across the room and took the seat the maid had abandoned, taking her hand. "Oh, Eliza, are you well? I feared the worst when Mr. Darcy said you were quite injured."

"I fell down a hill." Lizzy sighed, wishing she could confide in Charlotte. She would eventually, but now wasn't the time. "It was a disaster, and I have sprained my ankle. Worse, I have a concussion, and the apothecary insists I must remain here for a few days."

She grimaced at the thought, recalling how her poor sister Jane had been similarly forced to impose upon the courtesy of Netherfield. She had a new appreciation for her sister's position. "It is most obvious I am not welcome here, at least by Lady Catherine. Mr. Darcy can hardly be pleased to have me here either."

"Mr. Darcy seemed quite concerned about you," said Charlotte with a hint of tartness. "I think you are underestimating him. You have a tendency to minimize anything positive to do with him, particularly when it comes to attributing emotions to the man."

"That is because I have only ever seen him exhibit a few emotions, mostly pride or hauteur, and the occasional anger interspersed just for variety."

Charlotte seemed to lose the battle with her amusement, and she giggled for a moment before her expression became more severe again. "You are terrible, Eliza. Did he not come to your assistance?"

"It was the least he could do since he caused the predicament." Lizzy bit her tongue. "Never mind. I shall tell you all about it when I am back at Hunsford."

Her friend was obviously curious, but she accepted Lizzy's word on the matter. "I will ensure some of your things are brought over here to make you more comfortable, and I will visit you daily."

Lizzy grinned. "No doubt, Mr. Collins will insist on accompanying you so that he might bask in more time spent in Lady Catherine's presence."

Charlotte's lips twitched again as she shook her head. "You really are awful." She spoke with strong affection. "Is there anything I can get for you now?"

"No, I would simply like to rest. I have already taken the first dose of medication the apothecary left for me, and I am growing weary."

"I shall leave you then, but I will return with your items later." Her friend stood up, squeezing Lizzy's hand as she did so before taking a step back. "Rest well, dear Eliza."

Lizzy murmured a reply, not entirely certain it was coherent, as she allowed the need to sleep to slip over her once more.

"WAKE UP, MADAM," SAID a formal voice.

Lizzy somehow managed to peel open her eyelids and glare up at the offending voice that was trying so hard to wake her. "What do you want, Mr. Darcy?"

"The apothecary said we should check on you every few hours even if you are sleeping. I am to look at your eyes and make sure you are awake."

"I am certainly awake now," she said with a huff of protest, struggling to keep her eyes open as he bent closer. He was visibly peering into her eyes, but Lizzy was disconcerted by the strange thought that she wouldn't have to move much at all to press her lips to his. What a bewildering idea, to imagine kissing Fitzwilliam Darcy. Her brain must be truly scrambled from her injury to have such a crazy, imprudent idea occur to her.

"Your pupils appear the same size now. I was told to watch for that. I believe you can go back to sleep."

"Finally," said Lizzy with a hint of impatience as she closed her eyelids. She thought she heard the chair squeak slightly, indicating Mr. Darcy sat by her bed, but she couldn't find it in her to open her eyes to make sure. Once more, she slept.

THAT SET THE TONE FOR the next day or so, until Lizzy was finally able to maintain consciousness for more than a few minutes. Her head still throbbed, but her stomach felt calmer, and she was more aware of the ache in her ankle as well. All in all, she was quite miserable, so she decided books would be the panacea she needed.

When Mr. Darcy came to visit her that afternoon, as he was wont to do despite her insistence that he needn't bother, she asked, "Would you mind bringing me a selection of books from the library?" She uttered the request in response to his offer to fetch anything she might need.

"I would be delighted."

To her surprise, he left the room right away. Lizzy wasn't certain if something else had caught his attention, or if he'd simply left to run the errand. She prevaricated between being relieved to be rid of him and a vague ache of dissatisfaction to have him gone. Whatever was wrong with her? She attributed it to the lingering ailment of her head injury.

He returned a short time later with a stack of books. Lizzy appreciated his solicitousness in reading them off to her, and she selected a treatise on women's rights by Mary Wollstonecraft. He appeared slightly askance at that, but he handed her the book without comment, and Lizzy opened it.

She had every intention of reading and ignoring his presence until he got the message and left, but as she stared at the page, she was disconcerted to realize the words still blurred before her. Trying to focus on them and concentrate only made her headache worsen. With a sigh, she closed the book and set it aside.

"Miss Wollstonecraft does not appeal to you after all?"

"On the contrary, I have heard she has quite sensible ideas. Unfortunately, I cannot focus on them at the moment. The words are blurry." There went her great idea of occupying herself. She supposed she could spend more time sleeping, but that was quickly growing boring.

"This is the book you are set on reading?"

She turned her head to look at him as he removed it from her lap. "It is. I suspect it would not matter if I switched to a different book though. All the words are going to blur right now."

He nodded, opening the book and starting to read aloud.

Lizzy was shocked. "What are you doing, Mr. Darcy?"

"I am reading to you, Miss Bennet." He resumed the narrative.

She listened for a moment before shaking her head. It still caused a sharp pain, but it didn't make the world tilted around like it had the day of her injury. "You do not need to do that, Mr. Darcy. It is hardly necessary for you to keep me company, particularly since it is somewhat scandalous for you to do so."

He made a scoffing sound. "Nonsense. Millicent, the maid who sat with you the other day, is right outside in the hallway."

Lizzy turned her gaze to the door, seeing Millicent sitting across from them. The maid wasn't actually looking at them, with her head bent as it was over her sewing project, but her presence provided all the respectability needed to allow him to sit and read to her. She started to think of another reason to protest, but she was too tired to bother.

Besides, she did want to hear Miss Wollstonecraft's thoughts on women's rights. She couldn't deny a little part of her enjoyed making Mr. Darcy read such a book aloud to her anyway. She doubted he'd ever contemplated having to do so.

Before he could resume reading, she asked, "I take it you have no interest in reading this volume, Mr. Darcy?" She sounded entirely too polite when she asked, which must have revealed her intent to needle him.

He looked up at her and blinked, but his lips twitched. "Not at all. I have read it in the past, and it raises some interesting points, but I do believe Lady Louisa Burgess does a better job of expounding on how women might claim a more equal role in society and government."

Lizzy was literally stunned speechless. She had no idea how to respond to that, and as much as she hated to give him the satisfaction, she subsided into silence while he continued to read. He made it through two chapters before she started to get tired again, and when her eyelids closed, she heard him say, "I shall return to read more later, Miss Bennet."

"Thank you, Mr. Darcy," she said, and there was genuine gratitude in her tone. As much as she was loath to admit it, she appreciated his attempts to keep her entertained, and how he had gone out of his way to ensure she received proper care after the injury. Of course, it was the least he could do, since he had been the reason she had fallen to start with, driven by such anger to ignore her own safety to escape him.

HE RETURNED LATER THAT evening as promised, once more reading from Mary Wollstonecraft's book until Lizzy interrupted him. "Mr. Darcy, may I ask you something?"

He looked startled as he closed the book and glanced at her. The oil lamp he was using for illumination accented the planes and shadows of his face, making him even handsomer than usual. It was dreadfully unfair and quite distracting, particularly coupled with the lazy disarray of his curls from him having run his fingers through them a few times absently while reading.

She blinked, forcing herself to focus on the topic she wished to discuss. He appeared to be bracing himself, and she imagined he expected her to mention Jane again. Instead, she said, "We have a mutual friend... Mr. George Wickham?"

He scowled, anger replacing his trepidation. "Unfortunately, we do, though I do not call him friend."

Lizzy frowned, biting back an instinctive protest at how unfair he was. "I would consider Mr. Wickham a friend."

"Would you? He is quite good at making friends, though not quite so adept at keeping them once they become aware of his true nature." His eyebrows settled into a heavy line as he scowled.

Lizzy opened her mouth to defend Mr. Wickham, but she didn't want to argue with Mr. Darcy. Rather, she wanted to understand the animosity he felt toward the other man. "I understand your father showed a strong preference for him, and that must have been quite difficult for you as a child and a young man, but you are an adult now. Is it not time to move past that petty rivalry?"

His scowl deepened, and he drew in a shaky breath. He seemed to be counting silently to himself, perhaps in a bid to control his anger. "I do not know to what you allude, Miss Bennet." The words were delivered in a starched tone.

"I refer to your insistence on cutting him out of your life and denying him the living your father left him. Those are the petulant actions of a young child or adolescent, not a fully grown man old enough to administer an estate like Pemberley. It is beneath you to behave in such a way, Mr. Darcy." There was a gentle hint of chiding in her tone.

He scowled. "You must tell me what Mr. Wickham has relayed to you." He sounded surprisingly neutral as he made the request.

Lizzy scrunched her brow, struggling to recall his exact words. She couldn't entirely, so she would have to settle for paraphrasing. "Mr. Wickham shared with me that he was your papa's ward, and they were quite close. He expressed regret that Mr. George Darcy occasionally seemed to prefer him over you and made it show. He was quite aggrieved that it caused a rift between the two of you, and of course, he felt it bitterly unfair that you had denied him the living your father promised as vicar of Kympton because of your ill will and hurt feelings."

Mr. Darcy surprised her by laughing. True, there was a bitter edge to it rather than true amusement, but she had expected scalding anger or bitter defensiveness. His cold amusement was a shock.

"Papa occasionally seemed to prefer George to me, but that was not the cause of our problems. He and I were close, much like brothers, and we had a similar upbringing. My father sent him to Oxford along with me, planning to educate him to become the vicar, as he mentioned to you."

Lizzy nodded, since his part of the narrative agreed with what Mr. Wickham had shared, much to her surprise. She'd expected Mr. Darcy to spin it in a different way.

"It was at Oxford that I first realized how unsuitable Mr. Wickham would be for the position of vicar. He was a scoundrel, in short. He drank deeply, gambled away his allowance, and seduced girls of little consequence compared to his station. He ruined more than one young lady who had no recourse to go after him. I did try to warn Papa, but when I brought it up with him, I could see the topic was hurting him, so I changed the subject and never spoke about it with him again. I knew he would be a terrible choice, and I decided I would not give him the position of vicar upon Papa's passing."

Lizzy frowned, not quite sure she could reconcile the picture Mr. Darcy painted with the man she knew. "That seems quite unlikely to me."

He scoffed. "Does it? Is he not the same man who was being quite friendly with you only to announce his engagement to Miss King to your complete surprise?"

Lizzy flushed, feeling a stir of anger and embarrassment at the reminder. "How did you hear about that?"

"Gossip moves quickly, particularly in a backwater like Meryton. Even as outsiders, the Bingleys and myself heard about that."

She burned with humiliation as she looked away. "It was not like that. I had no expectations from him. I was simply surprised by his engagement."

His expression revealed his doubt. "No doubt it came as a shock, for he had perhaps indicated he had high regard for you." He sounded surprisingly understanding.

Lizzy looked at him, confused. "So, you denied him the living because you found him unsuitable?"

"Yes, but I did not cast him away with nothing. I gave him a check for three thousand pounds, which you will agree was a considerably generous compensation for not making him vicar, particularly after he expressed reservations of holding the position as it were. Mr. Wickham himself decried his ability to be an effective clergyman."

Lizzy's lips parted in a gasp. "You gave him money and did not just turn him out?"

"Indeed, though I have little doubt he has spun you an entirely different narrative." He shook his head. "He has a way of persuading people, and of dripping subtle poison in their ears. You are not the first to misjudge him and will not be the last. Even when he returned after frittering away his first three thousand pounds, I gave him another smaller payoff out of sentiment and our shared past. However, when he showed up for the third request, I had to cut him off."

Lizzy's mouth dropped open. "He managed to waste such a sum in just a few short years?"

"Barely a year," said Mr. Darcy, and he seemed sincere when he uttered the claim. "I was shocked but sympathetic, assuming he had simply lost control of any good judgment in the face of having such a sum at such a young age. Yet when he did it again, I could not continue to enable him. At that point when I refused him, he vowed I would be sorry. It was not long before he started plotting against me, though it took a few years for his plan to come to fruition."

Lizzy frowned. "What plan?"

"I am certain you have heard mention of my dear sister, Georgiana?" At Lizzy's nod, he said, "When she was fifteen last summer, she requested a level of independence, so I allowed her to rent a house at Ramsgate and stay there with her companion, Mrs. Younge. The woman came highly recommended, but I suspect her references were forged, for she turned out to be scheming in conjunction with Wickham."

"Oh, dear." She braced herself to hear something horrible.

"She allowed the man access to my dear sister, and he convinced Georgiana they were in love and must elope. If I had not arrived for a fortuitous visit, and she had not felt comfortable confiding their plan in me, she would have come to ruin all for her thirty-thousand-pound dowry. When I made it clear to Wickham I would never release it to him under any circumstances, even if he found a way to trick my sister into marrying him, he departed never to be seen again."

She gasped, unable to doubt the veracity of his words or the deep sadness conveyed within them, and the hint of helplessness he must have felt on his sister's behalf. It was clear it still tortured him. "Your poor dear sister." Anger rose sharply, and she scowled. "I suppose I should have realized he was trying to manipulate me, Mr. Darcy. After all, why would he share rumors of all he had been through if he did not wish for others to know and see him as a victim? I feel like such a fool for believing him."

"Do not be so hard on yourself, Miss Bennet. As I said before, you are not the first to be fooled by him, and sadly, you will likely not be the last. He is a true scoundrel in every way, and it is for the best that you know now."

Lizzy nodded her agreement. How could she argue otherwise, for indeed, it was a blessing to know the kind of man Wickham truly was? Now, she was forced to evaluate Mr. Darcy through different eyes as well. If what Mr. Wickham had told her were lies and half-truths, that meant he wasn't nearly as callous a man as she'd considered him to be.

Yet, he was still intent on keeping Jane from Bingley, so he was the architect of her sister's broken heart. She might be predisposed to think kindlier of him now, but she could never have a truly good opinion of Mr. Darcy while he was able to so firmly stand between her sister and happiness.

Chapter Three

Over the next few days of her confinement to bed, Lizzy had the company of Mr. Darcy, who often read to her, and they managed to keep disagreements and quarrels to a minimum. After discussing Mr. Wickham, they had stayed deliberately away from controversial subjects, though Lizzy more than once wanted to implore him to reconsider his opinion of Jane.

It wasn't for her sake but for her sister's, because though Bingley was an affable fellow, Lizzy was afraid he would not be able to stand up to Fitzwilliam Darcy's objections, should they continue. Lizzy couldn't imagine being happy with a man who could be such milquetoast, but Jane loved Bingley, so she was determined to give them the best chance possible to be together.

Lizzy also found herself reluctant to disturb the peace between them, because when they got along, she was startled by just how well she and Mr. Darcy meshed. They had lively debates about literature and modern ideas, but to her surprise, they were more likely to agree about something than disagree on many topics.

During that time, she also started to forge a friendship with Anne, so it was with some sadness when Lizzy found herself packing her valise and preparing to return to Hunsford a few days after her injury. She should be happy to escape Rosings Park and Lady Catherine, and she was, but she would miss this extra time with Miss Anne, who seemed to be closely watched by her mother and her companion, Mrs. Jenkinson. Lizzy was certain that would inhibit whatever growing friendship was forming between them.

"I am happy to see you ready to go home." Anne spoke from the doorway, though she didn't sound particularly convincing.

"I am happy to be returning to Charlotte's home as well, but you must come visit frequently, and of course, I shall come to see you."

Anne smiled, her wan face gaining some color. "That would be lovely. Perhaps you and Mrs. Collins will come for tea tomorrow afternoon?" She lowered her voice to a conspiratorial tone. "Mama is entertaining others, so it would be just the three of us."

That enticed Lizzy to accept, and she quickly nodded her agreement as she stuffed the last of her items into the canvas bag. "I believe that is everything."

"I shall walk you to Hunsford," said Anne.

"You shall not," said Lady Catherine as she appeared in the hallway, watching Lizzy with her beady eyes. "You must have your rest, dear girl. I am certain Miss Bennet can find her own way home now that she is capable of walking again."

Lizzy wanted to spare Anne from an argument with her mother, so she quickly nodded. "Of course, Lady Catherine. I am confident I shall return to Hunsford without issue."

"In that case, you must relay an invitation for dinner tomorrow night."

Lizzy nodded, hoping by some stroke of luck she might be omitted from that.

"Of course, with you up and moving about again, you must come too, Miss Bennet." Lady Catherine issued the invitation, but it seemed to be more from obligation than any true desire to have Lizzy's company.

Lizzy bore her no ill will for that, for she felt the same way about Lady Catherine. Enduring the other woman's presence was a chore and brought no joy. Still, she could hardly refuse the invitation, particularly since her dear friend would be visiting, and Lady Catherine had provided hospitality for the last few days, albeit grudgingly. "That would be delightful." Somehow, she managed to sound almost convincing.

Without another word, Lady Catherine nodded to her and continued on, clearing the hallway.

Lizzy lifted her bag, and Anne fell into step beside her. "I can still walk back with you." There was a faint sizzle of defiance in her words, and her chin nudged up slightly.

She quickly shook her head. "I do not wish for you to have issues with your mother. Besides, perhaps you should rest."

"I am not half as sick as my mother believes I am," said Anne with quiet dignity. "It is just one more way for her to control me." She seemed on the verge of admitting something, and her mouth opened, her eyes sparkling.

"Are you ready to return to Hunsford already?" asked Colonel Fitzwilliam as he interrupted them.

"Yes, Richard, she is. Would you be so kind as to escort her home?" Anne looked vaguely disappointed.

Richard looked thrilled though, and he extended his arm. "I would be pleased to escort you."

Lizzy put her arm through his and walked along with the colonel, parting from Anne before they left the second floor and walked down the stairs. Soon enough, they were crossing Rosings Park's grounds, and the colonel smiled. "This reminds me of the few mornings we have walked together in the past, Miss Bennet, though hopefully without injury this time."

"Mr. Darcy is not here to cause me injury," said Lizzy without thought.

Richard paused, turning to look at her askew. "Are you implying my cousin injured you?"

Lizzy's eyes widened, and she hastily shook her head. "Oh, no, not at all. He and I were exchanging heated words, and I was not paying attention. It was my own folly that brought me injury, Colonel Fitzwilliam."

He breathed a sigh of relief, but he still looked troubled. "I fear I might have been the cause of your heated exchange."

Lizzy tilted her head slightly. "I fail to see how, sir. You were not there."

"I have since received an earful from Fitzwilliam about my indiscretion and talking out of turn. I felt much like a schoolboy being disciplined by the headmaster." His eyes twinkle as he shared that in a humorous tone that made Lizzy smile. "I did not realize when I revealed his meddling to protect his friend that it was to protect said friend from your sister. I have told Mr. Darcy that surely he must be mistaken, for I can scarcely imagine any sister of yours would be the grasping, scheming type."

Lizzy flushed, flattered by the words, though she read nothing into them. Even if the colonel was madly in love with her, and she knew he wasn't, he would never turn his back on duty and obligation to settle for her humble dowry that would require him to remain in the militia. She had little interest in him in that regard anyway, for he was a fine conversationalist and enjoyed walking with her, but there was no spark between them.

Unlike with Mr. Darcy.

The idea hung in her mind for a moment, and she was shocked by it. She nearly gasped out loud and shook her head in rejection of the notion, only managing not to make a fool of herself at the last moment. Such actions would've surely prompted a gesture of concern from the colonel, and she would've had a difficult time inventing a reason for acting so peculiarly.

"I thank you for thinking more highly of my sister than Mr. Darcy, and you have not even met her. I assure you, she is not what he believes her to be. Jane loves Mr. Bingley, and I believe he has great affection for her as well, though I fear it will not be enough to allow him to stand up to his friend if Mr. Darcy continues to voice objections."

After a moment, Richard sighed and nodded. "I fear you are right. Bingley is a good chap but is not made of sterner stuff like some men."

"Still, it is not your fault we argued. I appreciate you relaying the information to me, for it has made me resolved to ensure Mr. Darcy changes his opinion. I shall see to it if it is the last thing I do."

"Or he does," added the colonel with a chuckle as they reached Hunsford. He saw Lizzy inside, declined tea, and soon departed.

Charlotte spent the afternoon fussing over Lizzy, ignoring her insistence that she was much better now, and Lizzy submitted to her friend's care, recognizing Charlotte needed to feel useful, particularly since Lizzy had been cared for at Rosings Park the last few days rather than by Charlotte at Hunsford.

Fortunately, by the next afternoon, Charlotte seemed to have accepted Lizzy was feeling much better, except for an occasional headache when she tried to focus too long on words or a task, and she made no objection as the two of them set out for tea with Miss Anne. Charlotte seemed excited, and she confided, "I do believe this will be the first time I have had a chance to speak with Miss Anne alone. She is frightfully guarded, as though her mother believes she is too fragile for regular interaction."

"I have observed that as well. I think it would be beneficial for Miss Anne if you two can form a friendship."

Charlotte nodded. "I would enjoy it as well, for I have yet to make any close friends here at Hunsford." Charlotte looked melancholy for a moment. "I confess, when I steered Mr. Collins in my direction and happily accepted his proposal, I looked forward to having a household of my own to manage. That has been exceedingly pleasant, and even Mr. Collins himself is not quite as intolerable as I feared, but I do miss Lucas Hall, Meryton, and visiting you."

Lizzy tucked her arm through Charlotte's. "Oh, Lottie, I miss you a great deal as well. I have my sisters, and Jane and I are lucky to be quite close, but there is nothing quite as special as my dear friend. I do miss you, but I am happy you find pleasure in your existence here." She grinned. "And that Mr. Collins is not nearly as intolerable as we feared."

They were giggling as they approached Rosings Park, but Lizzy made an effort to appear dignified, as Charlotte did the same. The butler allowed them entry and directed them toward the correct parlor, and they were every inch the gently bred young ladies they had been raised to be. Or at least, they gave every appearance of being so.

Miss Anne was waiting for them, along with her companion. Mrs. Jenkinson was preoccupied with needlepoint, and she appeared quite engrossed by it. She was seated by the window to obtain the best possible light, so it gave the three of them some discretion as they sat down for tea near the fireplace across the room.

"Thank you for having us," said Charlotte.

Anne nodded. "I am pleased that you accepted. I look forward to speaking with you more, Mrs. Collins, in hopes we might find we have things in common. It never seems quite possible when you and Mr. Collins visit though."

"Indeed, if my husband is not talking, your mother is." Charlotte flushed slightly as she said that, looking like she didn't know whether to giggle or apologize.

Anne's wicked grin eased the tension, and she nodded. "I confess, it is quite startling to find someone almost as verbose as my mother. Mr. Collins has a singular ability to keep talking about any topic endlessly."

"Unless Lady Catherine cuts him off. She has a singular ability to silence Mr. Collins. It is something I have never witnessed before," said Lizzy with a small grin as Charlotte smiled indulgently.

"My husband does enjoy speaking. Fortunately for his friendship with Lady Catherine, he enjoys complimenting her almost as much. It is a match made in heaven."

"Frankly, I do not know how you stand my mother's meddling." Anne seemed like she might faint as she made the admission, lowering her voice before speaking again. "I am used to her running my life, but it must be quite upsetting for you, Mrs. Collins. She always has an opinion on everything, and woe be to us all if we do not follow it."

Lizzy nodded her agreement, though she would've never said so out loud unless Charlotte brought up the subject. She'd observed that for herself during her visit to Rosings Park, and it was an area where she sympathized greatly with Charlotte. Fortunately for her friend, Charlotte had much more patience and tolerance than Lizzy had ever possessed.

"I have only been married to Mr. Collins for a short time, but I do believe I am mastering the art of finding a way to make Lady Catherine believe I have agreed with her and then going my own way whenever possible."

"Look at you, as though butter would not melt in your mouth," said Lizzy with a chuckle at her friend's innocent expression.

Charlotte just smiled, clearly having no plans to deny Lizzy's teasing accusation.

That afternoon tea set the course of their friendship with Anne, which kept developing and deepening over the next two weeks as she frequently hosted them for tea. Many afternoons, they had to endure the presence of Lady Catherine as well, but since Lady Catherine rarely visited the rectory, many times, Anne came to them for tea instead. Lizzy was certain she had to sneak out to do it, which seemed unfortunate. From what she had observed, Anne was not all that ill. As the woman herself had claimed, she seemed to be more controlled than indisposed.

That afternoon, when Anne showed up, there was something different about her. Her cheeks were fiery, and she seemed angry. Lizzy shared a concerned expression with Charlotte as they sat down for tea, not missing the way Anne angrily stirred the metal spoon against the bone china, causing a scraping sound that made Charlotte wince

"Is something troubling you, Miss Anne?" asked Charlotte.

Anne hesitated, opening her mouth and then closing it again. She stirred for another half-minute furiously before setting aside her tea, making a small thumping sound as it landed on the table. Charlotte winced again but made no admonishment. "My mother. She continues to push the idea I will marry Fitzwilliam. It is abhorrent, for he is more like a brother than a lover." She shook her head. "If I must marry a cousin, I would sooner marry the colonel, but that is because he is more fun. I have no desire to marry either of them."

"Has Mr. Darcy asked for your hand?" Lizzy tried to deny her negative reaction to the thought, wanting to ignore the way her heart constricted in her chest, and the bitter surge of jealousy that crept up the back of her throat.

"No, and I do not believe he will. We have spoken about the matter before, and I genuinely believe Fitzwilliam is as uninterested in marrying me as I am in marrying him. It is purely a fiction of Mama's devising, but she clings to it and refuses to entertain any other ideas or thoughts. I am certain she would not even meet with Matthew, though he seems bent on trying." After a moment, she paled before flushing again. "Oh, you must forget what I just said."

Of course, that was impossible. Lizzy leaned forward as Charlotte did the same, lowering their voices to ensure Mrs. Tesch, Hunsford's housekeeper, didn't overhear any part of the conversation. "Who is Matthew?" asked Lizzy quietly.

Anne flushed brighter still. "I should not say."

"I hope you know us well enough by now to know we will maintain your confidence," said Charlotte in an encouraging tone.

Lizzy nodded. "We will not say anything to anyone, particularly your mother, but it is most unkind of you to leave us without sufficient information."

Apparently, Anne wanted to talk about him, for it took little coaxing to get her to do so. "Matthew owns a little farm a few miles away from here."

Charlotte frowned, pursing her lips for a moment while she looked upward, as though thinking. "Would that be Mr. Matthew Bridwell?"

Anne hesitated before nodding. "The very same. He is a young widower with two adorable little children who need a new mother." Anne blinked. "Matthew has indicated he would like to propose to me, and he is insistent upon speaking with my mother, but I have done my best to dissuade him thus far. I know she will not allow the match, and I fear she might do something to harm Matthew's livelihood if he approaches her."

"That is dreadful. You love this Matthew?" At Anne's nod, Lizzy frowned. "There must be a way for you to be together."

"We have discussed eloping. He would prefer to get Mama's agreement, and he refuses to see just how horrible she can be. I do believe I could persuade him that Gretna Green is the answer for us, but how would I ever get enough time alone to sneak away and have enough of a head start to reach Scotland and marry over the anvil before Mama caught up?"

"You would have to have your mother otherwise engaged, perhaps somewhere she thinks you are involved as well. It is the only way I fear you could have a wedding," said Charlotte.

Anne nodded her agreement, but they fell silent as Mr. Collins opened the door, shouting, "Mrs. Collins, bring your friend."

Lizzy and Charlotte exchanged surprised glances, setting aside their teacups and saucers as they rose to their feet. Anne accompanied them as they entered the entryway, surprised to find Mr. Darcy standing with Mr. Collins. Lizzy wondered if they had overheard any of their conversation, but she quickly forgot her thoughts when Mr. Darcy stepped aside to reveal Jane.

Lizzy's mouth dropped open, and she rushed forward to hug her sister. "Jane, what are you doing here? I thought you were still in London with Aunt and Uncle Gardiner. Was I not supposed to join you there after my visit to Hunsford?"

"Yes, that was the plan, but two of the children have come down with measles, and Aunt Gardiner could not recall if I ever had it. She was concerned that if I stayed, I might fall ill, so she had planned to send me home. I got the idea of coming by Hunsford instead." She looked vaguely anxious as she looked at Charlotte. "I hope you do not mind, Charlotte?"

She shook her head. "Of course not, Jane, though you will have to share with Eliza. The rectory is not overly large."

"That will be nothing new for us," said Lizzy as she tucked her arm through Jane's. "We share a room at Longbourn, after all."

Mr. Darcy cleared his throat then. "It is good to see you up and moving about, Miss Bennet. Have you healed sufficiently?"

Jane frowned. "Healed? What does he mean, Lizzy?"

Lizzy waved a careless hand. "I shall tell you all about it in a short time, dear sister." She nodded to Mr. Darcy, with her tone naturally cooling when she spoke to him. How could it not with the live reminder of Jane right there to force her to recall exactly what his attempts to stop the courtship with Bingley were costing her sister? "I am quite recovered. Thank you."

He nodded, looking pleased for a second before his expression became darker. "I am here to relay a dinner invitation to Rosings Park. I happened to see Miss Jane arriving."

"We would be delighted to accept, Mr. Darcy," said Mr. Collins. He seemed bent on talking off Mr. Darcy's ear as he put his hand on his shoulder, leading him from the rectory. If it had been anyone else, Lizzy might've had a shred of sympathy, but she rather enjoyed watching Mr. Darcy squirm under the loquacious attentions of Mr. Collins with no one to bring him to heel. Lady Catherine was the only one Lizzy knew who could manage such a feat.

She led Jane to the room they would be sharing in the rectory, apprising her of the injury Mr. Darcy had mentioned before taking a turn listening as Jane shared how her heart was still broken. She'd had yet to see Mr. Bingley again, and Miss Bingley had made it clear she was not welcome at the Bingley townhouse.

Lizzy was hardly surprised that Caroline Bingley had proven not to be the friend Jane had believed her to be, but she was still sad on her sister's behalf. "All is not lost," she said confidently. "We will find a way for you to reconnect with Mr. Bingley. I would not be at all surprised if Miss Bingley kept your presence in London hidden from him."

Jane frowned for a moment, but then she looked hopeful. "Do you truly believe that might be the case, Lizzy?"

"I would be quite confident in guessing so. She wishes to thwart the match between you. What better way to do that than to keep the two of you separated? If he knew you were in London, I doubt she could have managed such a thing. No doubt Mr. Bingley was kept in the dark too."

"I sincerely hope so, for my heart aches to see him again. I fear he does not want to see me though. What if I imagined the depths of his affection for me? His own sisters hinted that he was quite often fickle. Mrs. Hurst mentioned a number of young ladies with whom he had spent time with over the years during the London seasons."

"Mrs. Hurst was no more eager to have you join the family than Miss Bingley," said Lizzy more bluntly than she'd planned to. Seeing Jane's frown of confusion, Lizzy sighed softly. "You might as well understand why, Jane. They do not consider you of good enough stock, and Lord knows, Mama went out of her way to make a poor impression upon them just by being herself. I doubt it has anything to do with you personally, but they have decided our family is not good enough to be joined to theirs."

Jane looked outraged. "Why would they ever think that? I admit, Mama can be a trial at times, but she was never deliberately unkind."

"She was gauche and clearly interested in Mr. Bingley's annual sum. That would be enough to be off-putting, I imagine." Sometimes, Lizzy marveled at how sweet and naïve Jane could remain, because though she was older than Lizzy, she on occasion seemed like a babe in arms in comparison.

Jane would insist on seeing the best in everything though, and Lizzy had yet to decide if that was a flaw or an asset in her sister's character. Lizzy was determined to be jaded enough for both of them so that Jane would hopefully never have to change.

"I must simply persuade them to see otherwise. Assuming I can reconnect with Mr. Bingley, of course." Jane sounded discouraged about the possibility.

"We will find a way yet, dear sister." Lizzy patted her on the shoulder. "Have faith in that."

Chapter Four

Fitzwilliam hadn't missed the way Cousin Anne, Miss Bennet, and Mrs. Collins had become quite close, whispering quietly together. The quiet whispering had expanded to include Miss Jane Bennet, and he was concerned they might be conspiring about something. It made him suspicious enough to think they were all working to further Jane's goal to get Bingley to propose.

He could scarcely believe that of his cousin, but he had to admit he didn't know her as well as he used to now that they were both grown. They had been friends as children, but the years had separated them, along with different life experiences. He'd also spent time shunning her company in an attempt to dissuade Lady Catherine from her plan to join them in marriage. Now, he wondered if he had acted the wrong way, inadvertently distancing himself from Anne while trying to dissuade his aunt.

Had he left her vulnerable for scheming? As he hovered nearby that evening, listening to the women whisper while Mrs. Jenkinson played the pianoforte and Lady Catherine dominated the conversation with the sycophantic Mr. Collins, he overheard the words *elope* and *wedding*. It made his blood run cold, convincing him they were somehow trying to further the scheme to bring Jane and Bingley together.

He would not have it, so as soon as the little group broke apart, he approached Miss Elizabeth. "I have a book that might interest you." He spoke abruptly, turning to gesture to the wall of books at the other end of the room. It would provide some privacy for them while still maintaining propriety with the rest of the group nearby. He started walking that direction, expecting her to follow him. After a moment, he realized she wasn't and turned back to look at her. "Well?"

"Some people might ask," said Lizzy in a too-sweet tone.

He'd spent enough time with her to recognize that tone indicated she was angry or annoyed. Sometimes, it also exposed her sarcasm, but tonight she just looked irritated. He was feeling a similar emotion himself, but he strove for a polite tone. "Would you please escort me to the bookshelf so I may show you the book?"

She nodded her head and walked beside him, but not so close that he felt prompted to offer his arm. He suspected that was by her design, for his appalling affection for her remained despite his best attempts to eradicate it. If she'd been close enough, good manners and personal foibles would have compelled him to offer his arm, knowing that light touch would never be enough to satisfy him but happy to indulge in the sweet torture.

When they reached the bookshelf, he randomly selected a volume, discovering it was a work by Plato. He handed it to her.

She glanced at it. "I have already read this, Mr. Darcy. Did you wish to discuss it?"

"What I wish to discuss is what has you conspiring so quietly with my cousin. You will understand I feel protective of her."

She frowned. "Do you feel protective enough to marry her, Mr. Darcy?" She seemed unsettled to ask.

He felt equally unsettled hearing it. "What? Of course not. Anne is like a sister to me."

"I am certain she will be pleased to hear that, as will…" She trailed off, looking undecided.

"What?" He prompted after a moment of silence.

She bit her lip, still looking undecided. "You truly care about Anne and wish for her to be happy?"

He nodded. "Of course I do. What kind of question is that?"

"If I take you into confidence, do you swear to maintain silence about what I tell you? I ask because I think you might be useful, if we can figure out a role for you."

He frowned, prompted by curiosity to agree, though he disliked the idea of keeping secrets. "You have my word."

She breathed a sigh of relief as she turned her body slightly, and he realized she was angling so no one could see her lips move. "There is a gentleman who has offered for Anne, or shall if your aunt will agree, but Anne does not believe Lady Catherine would accept his offer. It is true he is of humbler means, but Anne has sufficient dowry for them, and she deserves a chance to be happy." She delivered that with an air of challenge, as though she expected him to protest.

He was temporarily stunned speechless, for he could scarcely imagine his mousy cousin skulking about engaging in a secret love affair. On the other hand, he couldn't disagree with Miss Bennet's insistence that Anne had a right to be happy. "How are we to know if this man is sincere and not just after Anne's inheritance?"

"We do that by trusting Anne's judgment." There was a tone of admonishment to her words, leading him to believe they weren't solely discussing Anna and her beau. "If you trust Anne, you will help her find this chance at happiness. As you are aware, it would be unwise for her to elope without marriage contracts in place to protect her, but she grows desperate enough to take that step."

He frowned in consternation. "That would be absurd. She has nothing to protect her if he does not turn out to be a good husband."

Lizzy nodded. "Precisely, but Anne believes that could never happen. She is convinced he is a good man, and he might well be, but you must admit it would be better if we could find a way for her to have a union with him that maintains contracts and your aunt's approval."

He snorted before he could think better of it. "That is one thing you are unlikely to obtain from Lady Catherine. She is an inflexible woman, and she has decided Anne and I will marry. There is nothing that will convince her otherwise. Still, I shall make an effort."

She looked frantic then. "You promised not to say anything. I have taken you into my confidence, and you gave me your word, Mr. Darcy."

He was angry at the impeachment of his honor, so he drew himself fully upright to glare down at her. "I gave my word and will abide by it. I will discuss the possibility with my aunt that she considers allowing Anne to be courted by someone. I will once again endeavor to make it clear to her that I have no intention of offering for Anne's hand. I doubt she wishes for my cousin to end up a spinster, and poor Anne has been on the shelf long enough. I will simply reason with Lady Catherine."

Lizzy looked skeptical, and he imagined rightfully so. He made it sound simple and straightforward, but he could scarcely imagine it really going that way. Still, he was determined to maintain his air of calm resolve and not reveal any hint that he questioned his ability to get his aunt to be reasonable.

She was still frowning, though she seemed less concerned now. "You swear you will not reveal Anne's secret?"

He sighed heavily, holding onto his patience as best he could. "Do you realize the depths to which you insult me by implying I will not honor my word, Miss Bennet?"

Her lips curled for a moment, and she was scowling at him. It was rather surprising when her expression relaxed slightly, and she said, "I am sorry. I should not question your honor, and I do so only because I am concerned for Anne. If your aunt finds out..."

"I understand it would be the end of Anne's chance of happiness. I will not be the one blamed for that, so again, I tell you that you have my word."

She looked relieved, and perhaps even a little hopeful as she smiled at him. "That is most unexpected, but I am certain Anne will be grateful for your assistance."

"And you, Miss Bennet? Will you be grateful?" His tone had dropped, and he was unable to resist the urge to turn the question into one of slight suggestiveness. By the way her eyes widened, and her nostrils flared, she wasn't completely immune to his tone or his meaning.

"Anne is a good friend, and I, of course, would be grateful as well if you assist her. Undeniably, that cannot compensate for the unhappiness you inflict upon my sister." With those words, she nodded to him, handed back the Plato tome, and returned to the group at the other end of the salon.

He watched her go, displeased by the reminder of the conflict that remained between them, and recognizing he had little choice. He couldn't stand by in good conscience and allow Bingley to make a disastrous match that would tie him to a woman who didn't love him even if standing between them kept him from the woman he…

He quickly cut off that thought, refusing to acknowledge the word. His feelings remained stubbornly unchanged, but he knew it altered nothing. There could be no future for them, both because of his concerns about her sister's intentions, and his objections to her family. He'd once imagined himself beneficent enough to look past those flaws, but cold reason demanded he could do no such thing.

Besides, he was no longer certain Miss Bennet would be grateful for his consideration in ignoring how unsuitable her family was. She seemed terribly protective of them, and if he uttered the speech he'd once planned, acknowledging all the reasons he shouldn't want to marry her before offering to overlook them, he was unsure she would react as he'd once imagined. Rather than throw herself into his arms in gratitude, she'd most likely throw him out of whatever room they occupied.

It was a blessing he hadn't uttered the proposal he'd intended to issue weeks before. He was grateful about that now, though his love for Miss Bennet refused to die despite his many attempts to destroy it.

HE HAD A CHANCE TO speak with his aunt the next afternoon, so he joined her for tea. It was just the two of them, for her companion was nowhere about. She seemed rather pleased to have him to herself, and he girded his loins for battle as she poured tea for them and handed him a cup.

"You seem as though something is on your mind, Fitzwilliam." She spoke with a sparkle in her eyes as she sipped from her teacup. "Perhaps you wish to discuss the future?"

He nodded, gripping the teacup tightly as he strove for an even tone. "Specifically, I am concerned about Anne's future. She has been on the shelf for quite some time, Lady Catherine. Do you not think it is time she married?"

His aunt surprised him by beaming. He hadn't ever seen her look so happy. "Yes, I quite agree it is time for Anne to end her spinsterhood. You believe she should marry then?"

"I believe she should be given an opportunity to find happiness. For many women, that culminates in marriage."

His aunt nodded, giving him a shrewd look. "It is about time, Fitzwilliam."

He frowned. "I... What?"

"You have certainly taken your sweet time to sew your wild oats, but I am glad you are finally being sensible about the situation. I see no reason for a long courtship, and I am quite good friends with the cousin of the Archbishop. There should be no impediment for a quick ceremony, and it will be good to see Anne married."

He scowled. "Lady Catherine, I believe you have misunderstood—"

She continued as though he hadn't spoken. "There are things we must arrange and quickly. Yes, I do believe it is quite doable. I shall see to the myriad details, and you must relate to Anne that I have given my permission and blessing."

Fitzwilliam felt a headache starting, and he rubbed the bridge of his nose for a moment. "Lady Catherine, you are not listening. I did not come to discuss my engagement with Anne."

"Of course not, for there is no reason to have the affair drawn out. We should be discussing your wedding instead."

Fitzwilliam wanted to continue to protest and try to clarify his true intentions, but he stiffened at the sound of a familiar voice in the hall. Recognizing it, he got to his feet, excused himself from his tea with Lady Catherine, and rushed into the hallway to find Richard greeting Charles Bingley.

"You made good time, old chap," said Richard with a grin.

Fitzwilliam frowned at the sight of Bingley. "What are you doing here, man?"

"Your cousin invited me," said Bingley with a grin as he pumped Richard's hand before turning to Fitzwilliam and patting him on the shoulder soundly. "It did sound like a jolly good time, particularly with a certain Miss Bennet visiting at Hunsford," he said with an air of defiance, clearly recalling Darcy's persuasions he'd employed when arguing with Bingley to depart Netherfield after the ball.

He frowned. "You must be on guard against Miss Bennet. She is as bad for you as she ever was, and her family is beneath yours in every way, Bingley."

"I listened to you at the time, but I have regretted it, Darcy." There was quiet confidence in Bingley's tone, as though he had reached a decision and intended to stick with it. "I have missed Miss Bennet a great deal, and she has been in my thoughts ever since I agreed to leave Netherfield. When I heard from your cousin that she was visiting nearby, I came immediately. You might not approve, but my heart seems to have settled fondly upon her, and I cannot turn away."

"You are a fool if you continue courting her, Bingley. She is out for your money and nothing more."

A gasp caught his attention, preventing Bingley from answering. Fitzwilliam looked up, his stomach sinking at the sight of Elizabeth and Jane Bennet standing in the hall at the doorway. Miss Jane looked stricken, and Miss Elizabeth just looked angry.

She turned on her heel and strode away, and Fitzwilliam was surprised to find himself following her. He should stay and try to keep Bingley from making a disastrous choice, but all he could do was focus on how angry and betrayed Miss Bennet had looked, and how much he wanted to banish those reactions to his words.

Chapter Five

Lizzy rushed from Rosings Park, breaking into a run as soon as she had cleared the building. It wasn't ladylike, but she didn't care. Angry tears burned her eyes, and the cool wind blowing in the late-spring day wasn't enough to shock her back to composure. She gathered her skirts as she ran, not wanting to be encumbered. She heard Darcy yelling behind her, but she ignored him, in no mind to face off with him yet again.

Instead, she struggled with a sense of betrayal she had no right to feel. After all, he had never made any concessions, and certainly, he had done nothing to make her believe he had changed his mind about her sister. Lizzy had allowed her own emotions to soften toward him in spite of his beliefs, not because of his actions.

When he had agreed to champion Anne's cause, she'd taken it as proof that perhaps he was changing. She had allowed her low opinion of him to rise, though she realized it had been doing so steadily since he had been so tender while caring for her after their argument. Learning the truth about Wickham had weakened her resolve against him even further, and Lizzy supposed she'd allowed his continued objections to Jane to lose some of their impediment to her growing feelings.

With Jane far away, along with Bingley, it had seemed more abstract. However, the sharp reminder that nothing had changed still managed to shock her, and now it cut through her as her chest ached with unshed tears.

Lizzy found she couldn't run anymore, so she collapsed against a tree, hoping it would shield her from Mr. Darcy. Surely, he had given up trying to get her attention. She could scarcely imagine the starched and proper gentleman abandoning any thought of his image to run after her, so it was somewhat of a shock when his hand touched her shoulder a few seconds later.

She jumped in surprise as she turned to glare at him. "Why will you not leave me alone?"

"I cannot." He sounded almost broken as he made the confession. "Seeing your pain undoes me, Lizzy."

She stiffened at the use of her first name, knowing she should rebuke him for such familiarity, but she was in no state of mind to do so. "How can you be so cruel? I have assured you repeatedly that Jane cares deeply for Bingley, and yet you still plot to keep them apart."

"Just as you scheme to get them together. How can I trust your assertions about your sister when you have acted so dishonorably?"

Lizzy shook her head. "I do not know of what you accuse me, but you are wrong, Mr. Darcy."

His arms crossed over his chest. "You claim to have no knowledge of Richard's actions?"

Lizzy frowned. "I do not know what you mean."

"After you neatly maneuvered it so that Jane would visit at Hunsford, my cousin rushed to tell Bingley that Miss Jane was here. You are claiming you did not work with him on the matter?"

She glared at him. "I did not. The colonel did tell me he thought you had misjudged my sister, and his opinion was based solely on the strength of my character. Perhaps he was trying to right a wrong. You would have to ask him about that." She turned away from him. "I would work with him or anyone else to ensure Jane's happiness, but he is acting alone."

"I do not like the idea of you working with him." He spoke stiffly.

She shrugged a shoulder, still refusing to look at him. "I suppose I do not care what you like, Mr. Darcy."

"Yes, and that breaks my heart."

She wiped the tears that were streaming from her eyes before turning back to face him. "I must suspect you do not have a heart, Mr. Darcy, for you can consign my sister to such unhappiness based on snap judgments and the actions of others."

He looked unsettled, and perhaps he was actually reevaluating his words. He sounded like he was entering uncharted territory when he said in a grudging fashion, "It is possible I have misjudged her."

"More than possible. It is a certainty." She spoke strongly as she made the declaration.

He still looked uncomfortable. "I will agree to reevaluate my opinion based solely on their interaction and keeping in mind your contention that Miss Jane is just shy and reserved. If I have jumped to the wrong assumption, I will do my utmost to correct it."

Lizzy felt a tentative touch of hope, though she couldn't bring herself to smile. She did soften a little though. "I am certain you will reevaluate your opinion and discover the true goodness of Jane and the purity of her intentions toward Mr. Bingley if you do not view it through jaded blinders. Jane is the kindest and most caring woman I know, and she loves Mr. Bingley deeply. Surely, you will see that for yourself if you look at her without evaluating her through the lens of my mother or my family's background and unsuitability."

He nodded stiffly. "In return, you will refrain from plotting against me, particularly with Richard?"

A hint of exasperation tried to rise, but Lizzy did her best to breathe through it and sound calm. "I have already assured you there was no conspiring happening. Why does the idea of me working with Richard bother you though?" She spoke his name deliberately, quite enjoying the way Mr. Darcy's eyes flared, and his brows drew together. He appeared angry that she would address his cousin so casually, and Lizzy thrived on that, though she refused to examine why.

"I do not like the idea of you being so close to Richard."

She frowned. "You must know I have no designs on the colonel. Even if I did, the reality of the situation would prevent anything even if I had great affection for him. He would never return it."

His tone changed, becoming gravelly and hoarse. "Do you have great affection for Richard?"

Lizzy's pleasure in his suffering apparently had boundaries, because she quickly shook her head. "He is a kind man, and I consider him a friend, but nothing more. I do not have great affection for Colonel Fitzwilliam."

"I am pleased to hear that." He didn't further enlighten her as to why, and his ruddy cheeks indicated he found the topic of conversation uncomfortable. Since Lizzy did as well, she was happy to abandon it when he offered his arm, and they returned to Rosings Park without speaking again.

THE DINING TABLE AT Rosings Park was quite full that evening with the addition of two new guests. Lizzy sat beside Jane, who sat opposite Charles Bingley, and they both grinned at each other like besotted fools. Perhaps Lizzy should encourage Jane to do a better job of shielding her emotions, for it was quite unseemly to stare at the object of her affection so blatantly, but Lizzy was certain it would only further her cause. Once Darcy accepted Jane's regard was genuine, he would withdraw any objection, and her sister would be happy.

That would remove Lizzy's own objections to Mr. Darcy, and she realized that was perhaps a dangerous thing. In many ways, and in most that mattered, Mr. Darcy was an eminently suitable partner. Somehow, she had found herself softening toward him despite his continued objections to Jane and Bingley. Hearing his thoughts earlier had left her hurt and aching to realize he hadn't reevaluated them in spite of getting closer to her, but if he could find it in his heart to change his mind about

Jane, for her sister's sake, Lizzy was optimistic that perhaps it might give her a chance with Mr. Darcy.

A chance to do what, she didn't delve into further, not yet wishing to explore that uncomfortable avenue of thought when they had seemed like they would be enemies forever upon first meeting. Now, she dared think they might call themselves friends. Could there be more? She was both terrified and exhilarated at the idea of exploring the option.

"I have an announcement," said Lady Catherine, cutting across the conversation. Everyone reflexively fell silent, and Lizzy turned to look at the older woman, seeing a smug and satisfied smile that sent a chill through her, though she wasn't certain why.

"It gives me great pleasure to share the news that my nephew, Fitzwilliam, has finally offered for my daughter's hand. Join me in wishing them every happiness in the world." It was more of a command than a suggestion.

Lizzy's mouth dropped open, and her stomach twisted into knots as she stared at Fitzwilliam, who looked unsettled, before turning her gaze to Anne, who appeared aghast.

"Lady Catherine, that was not—"

The older woman cut across her nephew's attempt to speak. "I have already sent word to the Archbishop that we require a special license, and I foresee no difficulty in obtaining one. Preparations are underway for the wedding in four days."

"This is indeed magnificent news," said Mr. Collins, puffing up like a toad. "It will give me great pleasure to officiate the ceremony of two such wonderful people of quality. I can see the love between them, and I have no doubt it will last a lifetime."

In spite of her shock and ill feeling, Lizzy shot a disbelieving look at Mr. Collins, wondering how he could say such a thing with a straight face. She could see different emotions reflected on Anne and Darcy's face, but she wouldn't have called either one of them love or happiness.

They both looked vaguely ill, and Anne seemed bordering on the edge of anger. She clasped her goblet in her hand, squeezing hard enough that Lizzy feared the glass might shatter. "It would be nice if you had consulted with me about my future, Mama." She glared at Fitzwilliam. "And you, Fitzwilliam."

"Anne, I—"

"Nonsense. You have known this was the plan for years, Anne, ever since you were both in leading strings. Do stop being so contrary and enjoy your victory."

"If you will excuse me, my *victory* has left me with a terrible migraine." Anne forced those words through gritted teeth as she stood up and walked away from the table, ignoring Lady Catherine's admonishments to return. She kept her shoulders straight and her spine stiff as she exited the room.

Lizzy stood up almost immediately. "I shall check on Miss Anne."

"So will I," said Charlotte.

After a moment, Jane tore her gaze away from Mr. Bingley, who had been looking at her just as raptly. She cleared her throat and said, "I should come with you."

"I have never seen such terrible behavior," said Lady Catherine with disgust as the three of them departed the table without so much as a "by your leave" or an apology.

They found Anne in the sitting room of her suite, and she was rocking back and forth in a chair as she stared out the window into the darkness. "How has this happened? I cannot believe Fitzwilliam would do this to me. He assured me repeatedly he had no intention of marrying me. I never wanted to marry him either, and I will not."

"You will not have to," said Lizzy with confidence. That it was feigned confidence wasn't something Anne needed to know.

Anne looked at her, looking surprised. "I do not see a way out of it if Mama has already arranged for a special license, and Mr. Collins is prepared to officiate."

"I will concede there is no immediately clear way out, but we will find one. You will not be forced to marry a man you do not love at the expense of giving up a man you do. We must all put our heads together and find a way out of the situation." Her confident tone remained unwavering, and Lizzy was gratified to see the hope and burgeoning confidence in her friends' faces around her. It was daunting to be the source of inspiration, particularly since she had no idea how they were going to fix this, but she was determined they would find a way.

Chapter Six

Fitzwilliam had to wait two days before he had a chance to speak with Lizzy alone, for she seemed to be going out of her way to avoid him. No doubt, she thought he had betrayed her and lied to her, and he was determined to fix that impression as quickly as possible. Yet she proved elusive, much to his annoyance.

In the interim, he was provided ample opportunity to watch the interactions between Bingley and Miss Jane. Particularly in unguarded moments, when they were unaware of being watched, he saw an entirely different side to Jane. Her affection shone through, and he was reluctantly forced to admit he'd been wrong. Knowing that, he approached Bingley before he got a chance to speak with Lizzy, who was still evading him.

"I suppose you have come to warn me away from Miss Jane again," said Bingley when Darcy tracked him to the river that ran through Rosings Park. His friend was fishing, and Fitzwilliam was slightly wounded that Bingley hadn't invited him to come along. It was a testament to how deeply annoyed his friend must be with him, since he knew what an avid fisherman Fitzwilliam was.

Without looking at his friend, he claimed a second pole and started putting on the bait. "I have come to tell you I was wrong."

Bingley reared back, clutching his chest with his hand in an exaggerated fashion. "I apologize, but I must have misheard that. Would you say what you said again, but louder this time?"

"I was wrong," said Fitzwilliam after he cleared his throat, speaking more forcefully.

Bingley put his finger in his ear, twisting as though clearing any wax blockage. "No, that is what I thought I heard. Yet it cannot be, for you are Fitzwilliam Darcy, and you are infallible. I do not believe I have ever heard you admit you were wrong about anything. Did I mention ever?"

Fitzwilliam gave his friend a sour look, but he endured Bingley's shenanigans for a moment before saying, "I am certain I have been wrong before, though I must admit, I might not have confessed to that state in the past. You know my upbringing, Bingley, and how I was encouraged to be kind to servants and those beneath me, but there was never any doubt Darcys enjoyed an exalted position above them. I fear that has spilled over even into my friendships with equals."

"I would be happy to refute that claim, if I could," said Bingley with a small smile.

"I have a frightful tendency to decide on a course of action and stick with it until I have forced others to comply. When it comes to Miss Jane Bennet, I believe I was wrong. She is not grasping for your fortune. She appears to genuinely adore you." He arched a brow as he looked at his friend, deciding to reciprocate. "Heaven knows why she has reached such a strange conclusion, but she finds you a pleasant enough fellow. I suppose I must feel sorrow for her, for she appears quite willing to join her future to yours."

Bingley burst out laughing. "Do not try to distract me with your own barbs, Fitzwilliam, for I fully intend to enjoy the moment of you admitting you were wrong. However, I will further enjoy the moment by approaching Miss Jane and asking to court her."

"I am certain you will find a receptive audience. I wish you much happiness, my friend." He was completely sincere when he said the words.

Bingley looked unexpectedly serious for a moment as well. "Perhaps you have not yet completely ruined all chances for your own happiness, Darcy."

He frowned. "Whatever do you mean, Bingley?"

"I mean the other Miss Bennet. She is not quite as charming as Miss Jane, but she seems to suit you well enough, and you have not been successful in hiding the depth of your affection for her, except perhaps from the lady herself. So, I will wish you well as well."

He could have protested, but what was the point? Bingley had moments of perceptiveness that sometimes startled Fitzwilliam. Why deny his friend the moment and the acknowledgment? "I fear I might have bungled that so entirely that she will never see me in such a light."

"The only way to know for sure is to speak with her." With a whoop of joy, Bingley suddenly dropped his fishing pole. "I swear, I have no patience for this now. I must speak with Miss Jane immediately." He gestured for his valet, and Higgins stepped forward. "Do see about tidying up this mess, please, Higgins?"

He didn't wait for the valet's acknowledgment as he turned to Fitzwilliam. "I am off to see my lady and suggest you do the same." With a clap on his shoulder, Bingley darted away.

Fitzwilliam couldn't find quite the same level of joy or excitement in doing so, for the prospect of facing Lizzy and apologizing for everything that had gone wrong sat heavily on his pride, but maintaining his ego seemed like small recompense when compared to the possible reward of gaining Lizzy's love and affection.

He found her almost an hour later, not really surprised that she had been walking the grounds and had paused to sit on the grass under a tree to read. She seemed startled to see him and more startled when he sat down on the ground beside her.

She looked at him, and though her expression was cool, he didn't think she was entirely unwelcoming. "What do you want?"

"I have come to apologize."

"I fear you shall have to clarify for what, Mr. Darcy, for that list could potentially be endless."

He chuckled in spite of himself, finding it enchanting the way she managed to tear him down, though he rarely felt truly deflated. Her sharp tongue was one of the things he quite liked about her, which indicated he must truly be a man in love, for otherwise, it would surely prove irksome.

"The first apology I must make is for misjudging your sister. I have already said as much to Mr. Bingley, but I now know I was wrong, and I withdraw any objections. Even now, Bingley is probably finding Miss Bennet, or has already done so, and has entreated her to accept his courtship."

"I am well pleased to hear that, Mr. Darcy." She gave him a genuine smile. "It is good to know you are capable of reevaluating even the most incorrect of opinions."

He laughed as he shook his head. "I must also apologize for the muddle with Anne. I truly did not offer for her hand. I have tried to explain that to Lady Catherine, but my aunt refuses to hear me." As he spoke, he cautiously reached for Lizzy's hand, which rested on her knee. Though both their hands were gloved, there was still a certain intimacy in the act of holding her hand, and he reveled in it, particularly when she didn't pull away.

"We were angry with you to start with, thinking perhaps you had fooled Anne, but we soon realized it was probably just such a situation. Anne is convinced you have no desire to marry her."

"No, I do not." Still holding her hand, he brought it to his lips and kissed the back of her glove. "There is another lady I would much prefer to marry, though I suspect she will make me work hard for that agreement, and we will have perhaps a long and fraught courtship."

"Perhaps the lady will surprise you and let bygones rest in the past. Perhaps she will not be eager for a drawn-out courtship either, Mr. Darcy."

He looked up at her, captivated by the way her eyes sparkled and the knowing grin on her face. "To have such an outcome is more than I could hope for, Miss Bennet"

"I do not object if you call me Lizzy in circumstances such as these, Fitzwilliam." She seemed to be trying out his name, and apparently, she liked it, for she nodded.

He smiled his approval. "In that case, I shall revel in calling you Lizzy. Perhaps someday, I will call you my Lizzy."

She smiled for a moment, but then her expression faded to one of concern. "First, we must extricate you and Anne from the situation of your making and allow her to be happy."

"I fear it is too late to prevent the ceremony. Lady Catherine has obtained a special license, and Mr. Collins is prepared to go ahead."

"It is a singular opportunity to allow Anne a chance to get a sizable head start." Lizzy fell silent for a moment before turning to look at him in a considering fashion. "I do believe I have an idea, Mr. Darcy. You will probably think it quite mad though."

"I am prepared to listen to any amount of madness that might spill from your tongue, Lizzy, and I fear I am so far gone, I will likely embrace it."

She looked slightly disgruntled, but after a moment, she nodded and started to plan out loud. It was mad, but there was a certain brilliance to it as well, and he found himself readily agreeing. Her madness prompted a strong dose of his own, and he began to make pertinent plans of his own...

Chapter Seven

Fitzwilliam stood in the church two days later, with Mr. Collins behind him as he waited for his bride to appear. There was some nervousness, and he wondered if Lizzy's plan would go ahead, or if Lady Catherine would see through it and immediately stop the situation. Fortunately, his aunt seemed blissfully oblivious to their machinations, and she didn't blink an eye when his bride appeared with her heavy veil, walking down the aisle unescorted.

There was a difference in his nervousness as she reached him, putting her arm through his. He thought he saw a ghost of a smile through the veil, but with all the heavy lace, it was difficult to discern for certain.

As one, they turned to face Mr. Collins, who seemed like his eyes were shining with unshed tears. Perhaps he was reveling in Lady Catherine's perceived victory as well, and he clearly believed he was about to unite a happy couple. Fitzwilliam smiled at that, and Mr. Collins must have taken it as one of praise, for he beamed back before he cleared his throat and adopted a solemn expression.

"Dearly beloved, we are here to witness the joining of this man and this woman in God's holy union..."

He continued to drone on, and as he did so, Fitzwilliam grew tenser. He could feel his bride tensing as well, her fingers digging into his forearm as they approached the penultimate moment of the ceremony.

"Mr. Darcy, take Miss Anne's hand in yours and repeat after me."

Fitzwilliam cleared his throat. "I would be delighted, but as to that..." He trailed off as Lizzy lifted her hands to pull back the veil and reveal her face underneath it. "I could not solemnly promise to love and accept Anne when my heart fully belongs to another."

"What is the meaning of this?" demanded Lady Catherine as she surged to her feet. "What have you done, you wicked girl?"

"I have given Anne a head start," said Lizzy with aplomb, enduring the shocked whispers and muttered gasps behind them as people in the church reacted to the surprise revelation.

Catherine rushed forward. "A head start for what?"

"Anne had no desire to marry me, and I did not desire to marry her either, Lady Catherine." Fitzwilliam nodded to Mr. Collins, who looked like he was on the verge of apoplexy. "When you refused to listen, you drove us to this point. By now, I have no doubt my cousin is in Scotland about to be married over the anvil."

Lady Catherine scowled. "Married? To whom?"

"A fine young man," said Mrs. Collins from her spot on the second row of the bride's side. "If you give him a fair chance, I am certain you will like him, though we all agree that is unlikely. Giving him a fair chance, I mean," she added with a sparkle in her eyes.

Lady Catherine appeared bewildered. "You are part of the scheme as well, Mrs. Collins? I expected better from you." She turned to her favorite sycophant. "And you, Mr. Collins, surely you are not involved?"

"Of course not, Lady Catherine," said Mr. Collins with nauseating obsequiousness. "I would never plot against you, particularly knowing it is your heart's desire to have Anne happily settled with Mr. Darcy."

"Indeed." Lady Catherine snapped open her fan and started to fan herself. "I do not know what outrage is occurring, but I will put a stop to it. If Anne manages to succeed in her ghastly plan to elope, I will simply have the marriage set aside."

"It is my understanding Anne has reached the age of majority," said Lizzy, sounding too sweet. "There is little you can do to end the marriage."

"I shall disown her."

"That is your right," said Fitzwilliam as he crossed his arms over his chest, giving his aunt a scowl of disapproval. "Of course, that does not prevent her from inheriting from Uncle Lewis. She is past the age now to do so, and she gets everything, does she not, Lady Catherine? Including Rosings Park?"

His aunt's mouth dropped open, and for the first time, she looked ill-at-ease "I do not know what you are implying."

"I am merely pointing out the obvious—the home that you love will be Anne's to control as soon as she is married. Marriage circumvents her need to wait to gain control of her trust. It would behoove you to be supportive, or at least not be negative and try to ruin Anne's chances of happiness."

Lady Catherine looked like a swollen toad as she drew herself up in her outrage. "I have never been treated with such disrespect. Shame on you, Fitzwilliam, and that common trash beside you." She shook her head as she glared at Lizzy. "You will come to a bad end, girl. Mark my words."

Lizzy seemed remarkably unconcerned as she shrugged. "Perhaps," she said cheerfully. "At least Anne will not."

Without another word, clearly enraged beyond the ability to speak, Lady Catherine turned and strode from the church. Stunned silence followed for a moment, and then muttering started again.

Mr. Collins removed a handkerchief from his pocket and mopped his face, looking ill. "I cannot believe your audacity, Cousin Eliza. How could you do such a thing? You have brought shame to the family."

"Perhaps," said Lizzy, still sounding cheerful.

"I think she has behaved admirably, and she has done all this to ensure Anne's happiness. That should be paramount to you, Mr. Collins." Fitzwilliam couldn't help chastising the clergyman.

Mr. Collins looked temporarily bewildered as he blinked and shuffled. "I... As... Well..."

Lizzy turned away from him, clearly done considering Mr. Collins. She started to take a step down the aisle, and Fitzwilliam put his arm around her waist. She paused and looked at him with a frown. "What is it? I believe we have bought Anne sufficient time. Do you not think?"

"Indeed, but we are not yet finished, Miss Bennet." Seeing her look of surprise, he said, "While you have been busy with your plans, I have been doing the same." He lifted his voice and called, "Would you step inside please?"

He watched Lizzy instead of the entrance to the church as Thomas and Fanny Bennet appeared, followed by their other daughters. She looked shocked, vaguely appalled, and then happy yet confused. She took another step toward them, but Fitzwilliam tugged her back to stand beside him. "Wait, love, and they will come to you."

She was still clearly confused. "I do not understand."

"I have spoken to your papa and the Archbishop. Mr. Bennet was harder to convince than the Archbishop, believe it or not. I believe the elder clergyman has a sense of humor, for he quite enjoyed the tale when I told him of our plan. He happily changed the license and signed it, and Mr. Bennet eventually agreed as well. The contracts have been signed, save for the last one required if you say yes."

Lizzy frowned, obviously recalling he had disappeared the day before, telling her he had business to which he must attend. She had been engrossed in helping Anne plot this venture, so she hadn't asked too much, to his relief.

"Why are they here?"

"Why, to give you away, my dear," said Fanny Bennet with a hearty chuckle. "To a man who makes ten thousand a year. Think of what jewels and carriages you shall have, and the pin money."

Fitzwilliam winced slightly at the vulgar statement, as Lizzy did the same, but he mostly ignored it. Fanny Bennet was part and parcel of having Lizzy in his life, and it was a more than fair tradeoff.

"You are genuinely wanting to marry me? Today? Via a special license?"

It was difficult to tell how she felt about that, but he nodded as he gave her a solemn look. "It is my sincerest wish, and I hope you will agree. Will you marry me, Elizabeth Bennet?"

She looked around, as though trying to comprehend it all. When her gaze returned to him, her lips tightened for a moment before her chin wobbled, and then she started blinking. "This is simply mad, Mr. Darcy."

"Yes, but will you do it anyway? Will you do me the great honor of being my wife?"

It seemed like the longest moments of his life as he waited for her answer. With a small cry of joy, she embraced him, and he kissed her when their lips brushed together. It was no gentle kiss either. It was full of pent-up emotion and was the kind of kiss that wouldn't have been polite in any company, particularly since they weren't yet married.

That, coupled with Mr. Collins's squeak of outrage, forced him to pull back as he turned to face his aunt's vicar. "Will you marry us, Mr. Collins?"

William Collins seemed on the verge of refusing for a moment, but a glance at Charlotte made him deflate, and he nodded. "Of course, Mr. Darcy. It would give me great pleasure." He wasn't particularly convincing, but he was willing to do it, and that was good enough for Fitzwilliam.

Apparently, it worked for Elizabeth as well, because she put her arm through his, and they faced Mr. Collins again. Within moments, they had repeated their vows, shared a much more chaste kiss, and were presented as Mr. and Mrs. Darcy to the assembly.

His heart felt like it would burst from pride as he walked down the aisle with Lizzy's arm through his, knowing she was his wife. Where he had once thought he was lowering his standards to accept her, he now recognized that she was elevating his life in every way, and he was grateful she had agreed to do so.

He understood and recognized what a blessing Elizabeth Bennet was, and how close he had been to throwing it all away. He would never make that mistake again and intended to cherish her every day for the rest of their lives together.

Epilogue

More than a year later, the Bridwells arrived at Pemberley for a summer visit. Lizzy found Anne's darling stepchildren as adorable as she had claimed them to be in correspondences, and it was clear the two children had bonded well with their new mother. Anne seemed equally happy with Matthew Bridwell, and Lizzy was happy about that as well.

For her part, she had found the kind of happiness she'd only dared dream about, and there were still times it struck her as odd or even funny that her happiness could come in such a package as Mr. Darcy, who'd seemed so incompatible in every way, but now suited her quite perfectly.

Lizzy was mindful of her belly bump when she hugged Anne, who held her tiny infant son in her arms. They shared a knowing look that spoke of all the happiness they had found, and she valued Anne's friendship almost as much as she valued Fitzwilliam and the happiness he had brought to her.

"Is Lady Catherine making you miserable?" asked Fitzwilliam with a hint of protectiveness after he had kissed his cousin on the cheek.

"Not at all. She has tried, but we mostly ignore her attempts, and it helps that I do not live at Rosings Park with her now. She was scandalized when I chose to move with Matthew to the small house on the farm, but I find it a much more appealing existence than living in that cavernous home with my mother." There was a new confidence and air of happiness about Anne that was impossible to miss, along with a glow of vitality that had long been absent. She'd clearly found what made her happy and had no regrets.

Lizzy could relate as she snuggled against Fitzwilliam a short time later, after they had parted from the visiting family, who would rest for a while before dinner. "They seem quite happy."

"Hmm, yes, as happy as Bingley and Miss Jane, but I daresay, they cannot be as happy as us."

She frowned, intrigued by the claim as she looked up at him. "How did you come to that conclusion?"

"I believe it would be physically and spiritually impossible to be any happier than we are, and they would be breaking all sorts of rules of the universe if they somehow managed to surpass us."

She giggled as she shook her head at his fantastic words. "I suppose I agree with you. I do not see how anyone could be quite as happy as we are, darling Fitzwilliam." She lifted her head for a kiss, and he bent his head to oblige. It was certainly not the first time they had kissed, and it would not be the last, but each time felt as amazing as their first kiss, and she relished his arms around her and his lips over hers as she savored the moment with her husband.

PLEASE SIGN UP FOR Abbey's newsletter[1] to receive information about new releases. If you have any difficulties, email Abbey to request a manual add.

---

1. https://www.subscribepage.com/JAFF

About The Author

Abbey is a diehard Jane Austen fan and has loved Fitzwilliam since the first time she "met" him at age thirteen upon borrowing the book from the school library. He is the ideal man, though Abbey's husband is a close second. Abbey enjoys writing various steamy and sweet Jane Austen variations, but "Pride & Prejudice" (and Mr. Darcy) will always be her favorite.

Did you love *Follies & Foibles: A Sweet "Pride & Prejudice" Variation*? Then you should read *Darcy's Runaway Bride: A Sweet "Pride & Prejudice" Variation* by Abbey North!

A costly kiss...A moment of madness causes Lizzy and Fitzwilliam to be compromised. They reluctantly wed, but he believes she conspired with her mother to force the union. Under those circumstances, they will never make a marriage work, so she agrees to his plan to pursue an annulment in three years. Lizzy is humiliated but determined to live her life as though Mr. Darcy isn't part of it...and he isn't.Nearly four years later, an irate Fitzwilliam has come to America in search of his wayward bride. He wants to secure the annulment, so he follows her to the Colonies after she moves there when her sister marries an American. Bingley is along, and he doesn't hide his disapproval of Fitzwilliam's plan. When he finds Lizzy, she's quick to agree to the annulment as planned, so they undertake a journey to the nearest city to find legal counsel.Along the way, they are set upon by bandits. Barely escaping, Lizzy is perilously injured, and Fitzwilliam has to find them help. As Lizzy heals, he realizes he can't imagine living without her. Will Lizzy give him a second chance, or is she determined to end their marriage that has never really begun?

Also by Abbey North

A Month To Love
Reproach (Part One)
Resentment (Part Two)
Rapport (Part Three)
A Month To Love Compilation

Crime & Courtship
Rapacity & Rancor: A Pride & Prejudice Variation
Abduction & Acrimony : A Pride & Prejudice Variation Mystery Romance
Extortion & Enmity: A Pride & Prejudice Variation Mystery Romance
Murder & Misjudgment: A Pride & Prejudice Variation Mystery Romance
Perfidy & Promises: A Pride & Prejudice Variation Mystery Romance
Crime & Courtship: A Sweet Pride & Prejudice Mystery Romance Compilation

Darcy's Courtesan
Adversity (Darcy's Courtesan, Part One)
Avidity (Darcy's Courtesan, Part Two)

Amity (Darcy's Courtesan, Part Three)
Darcy's Courtesan: A Sensual "Pride & Prejudice" Variation

Marriage & Mysteries
Honeymoon & Hemlock

Mr. Darcy's Secret Stories
Mistaken Masquerade: A Pride & Prejudice Variation
Mischief & Matchmaking: A "Pride & Prejudice" Variation

Standalone
Christmas At Pemberley: A Pride & Prejudice Variation
A Scandalous Proposition: A Pride & Prejudice Variation
Shadow of Darcy: A Sensual Pride & Prejudice Paranormal Variation
Darcy's Obsession
Blackmailing Lizzy: A "Pride & Prejudice" Variation
Darcy's Wicked Game
Danger With Darcy: A Sensual "Pride & Prejudice" Variation
Passion & Prostrations: A Sensual "Pride & Prejudice" Variation
Darcy's Debt: A Sensual Pride & Prejudice Variation
Obstinacy & Obligation: A Sweet Pride & Prejudice Variation
Follies & Foibles: A Sweet "Pride & Prejudice" Variation
Heartsick: A Sweet "Pride & Prejudice" Variation
Darcy's Alibi: A Sweet "Pride & Prejudice" Variation
Darcy's Runaway Bride: A Sweet "Pride & Prejudice" Variation
Never A Bride: A Fade-To-Black "Pride & Prejudice" Variation
Marooned With Darcy: A Sensual "Pride & Prejudice" Variation
Compromising Mr. Darcy: A Steamy "Pride & Prejudice" Variation

Marrying Mr. Darcy: A Sensual "Pride & Prejudice" Variation
To Dance With Darcy: A Sweet "Pride & Prejudice" Variation
Darcys' First Christmastide